SLEEPING BEAUTY

There once lived a king and queen who were finally blessed with a beautiful and healthy baby girl after years of praying for a child. They were overjoyed and held a great feast to celebrate the christening.

All twelve fairies in the kingdom were invited. After the banquet they each gave the child a special present. One at a time the fairies bent over the

cradle and granted the tiny princess gifts such as beauty, wisdom, kindness, and courage.

The eleventh fairy had just completed her wish when, suddenly, a thirteenth fairy appeared in a swirling, icy wind, with black bats circling around her head. She was old and ugly, and she reeked of evil. The royal couple had forgotten all about her. For many years, the wicked fairy had lived far away, atop a distant mountain where she was never seen by anyone. Many believed that she was dead.

The ugly fairy was furious that she had been snubbed. "I have a gift for your little princess, too," she shrieked, waving her magic wand. "When she is sixteen years old she will prick her finger on a spindle and die."

She cackled and then vanished in another freezing gust of wind.

The chill that remained gripped the hearts of the king and queen. They held each other and wept, the joy of the day destroyed.

Then the twelfth fairy

stepped forward. "I am young and not as powerful as the evil one. I cannot undo her curse. But," she said quietly, "I can make it less severe." She held her wand high over the princess and offered, "When the princess pricks her finger she shall not die, but instead she will sleep for one hundred years, until the kiss of a good prince breaks the spell."

The king immediately proclaimed that it would be forbidden for anyone to have a spindle of any kind within his kingdom. Anyone found guilty would be put to death instantly. His heralds announced the message throughout the realm. Spindle burnings were held in town and village squares throughout the countryside. It took some time but, at last, the king was assured that not a single spindle was to be found anywhere in the land. The princess was out of danger.

As the years passed, the princess grew to have all the qualities the fairies had given her. She was beautiful, kind, intelligent, and generous. She was loved and admired by every-

one. A number of princes had asked for her hand in marriage, but she had refused them all.

In the early spring, on the morning of her sixteenth birthday, her parents took her to an old castle in the country. The journey was long. Then, the king immediately met in private with his advisors, and the queen had to meet with the palace staff.

All alone, the princess felt restless. She strolled through the garden, then wandered around the castle. She watched the cooks preparing a meal in the kitchen. She looked at paintings of her ancestors in the main hall. She was still bored.

She thought that perhaps she should have remained at home

and played with her ladies in waiting. But it was her sixteenth birthday and she wasn't supposed to be playing games any more.

She came to a small entryway at the far end of a long hall. A narrow spiral staircase led to the top of the tower. Brushing aside dust and cob-

webs, the princess climbed the steps and found a door slightly ajar. She looked inside. An old woman was sitting beneath the window, spinning wool. She had lived in the tower for years and had never heard the king's proclamation banning spindles. She greeted the princess with a shy smile.

The princess was no longer bored nor restless. Here was something she had never seen before. "What are you doing?" she asked the old woman.

"I'm spinning wool on my old spindle," the old woman replied.

"Is it fun?"

"It's a job like any other, my child," the old woman sighed.

"Is it difficult?"

"Oh, no, not at all," the old woman told her. "It's easy to learn."

"Then, please, may I try?" The princess asked so nicely that the old woman could not refuse.

The princess eagerly reached out to take the spindle, pricking her finger the instant she touched it. She fell senseless to the floor.

The panic-stricken old woman rushed for help. When the king and queen saw their unconscious daughter, they realized the wicked fairy's curse had come true.

They brought the princess back home and gently placed her on her own bed. They knew she was only sleeping, not dead, but still their hearts were heavy. Even if she did awake in one hundred years, all the people she knew and loved, and who loved her, would already be dead. What could they do?

Meanwhile, the fairy queen circled the castle, riding a firey dragon. With a wave of her magic wand, everyone in the castle fell into a deep sleep. Even the animals and the plants all slept. A thick forest of spiny trees and thorn bushes sprang up to hide and protect the palace.

While the castle slept, twenty, fifty, seventy, ninety years passed, and more. Then

one day, a prince who was hunting nearby saw a tower rising above the trees.

"Who lives in that secluded place?" he asked a farmer.

"Some say a dragon or an ogre roams those empty halls," came the answer, "but others say there is a beautiful princess inside."

The daring prince felt compelled to solve the mystery. For hours he chopped through thick brambles with his sword. At last a path was clear and he could see the great castle appear before him.

At first he did not notice anything odd. But when he walked around and inside the castle he saw people fast asleep in the most extraordinary places and positions. The cooks slept in the kitchen beside a roaring fire. Knights were sleeping outside, leaning on their swords. A jester slept on the steps, a mandolin in his hands, and elegant ladies slumbered together on a long sofa. Even the animals–two parrots in a gilded cage, a cat and a puppy on a rug, a fly poised on the rim of a glass–were asleep. The prince called out, but no one stirred. He tapped someone on the shoulder, but there was no change.

The silence made the prince shudder. It was eerie. He did not know what to think. But he was brave and continued to explore.

Before long he entered the princess's chamber. Lying peacefully on a magnificent bed, fully clothed, was the most beautiful girl the prince had ever seen. He could not

take his eyes from her lovely face. If only he could wake her!

He approached her. The nearer he got, the more beautiful she looked. Gently, he leaned over and brushed her forehead with a tender kiss. To his surprise, she opened her eyes, smiled, and threw her arms around his neck.

"Oh," she murmered, "It's been ever so long, my prince!" They both knew from that moment on, they would never be happy apart.

All the people in the palace, all the animals and the plants, awakened as soon as the princess spoke her first words. Everyone immediately rushed to the princess's bedroom. They were relieved to see her rosy-cheeked and healthy, embracing a handsome prince. The twelfth fairy had been successful after all!

With everyone looking on, the handsome prince asked the beautiful princess to marry him. Without hesitation she accepted, and her parents immediately gave their consent.

The loving couple were married a few days later, in the

most splendid ceremony anyone could remember. The newlyweds left soon afterwards for the prince's distant kingdom.

Within a few years, they had two children, a boy and a girl as beautiful, kind and generous as their parents. Everything was wonderful, except that the prince's mother was insanely jealous of her daughter-in-law and the children. She managed to hide her true feelings most of the time, and no-one suspected that anything was amiss.

When war came to the prince's kingdom, he had to go with his soldiers to lead them in battle. Worried about his family, he asked his mother to watch over his wife and children.

"Never fear, my son," the treacherous queen told her son. "I will take care of them." They wished each other well and the prince rode off.

It had, of course, occurred to the queen that this would be the perfect time to get rid of her daughter-in-law and the children once and for all. She summoned one of the royal cooks, a man she trusted who was de-

voted to her. "Kill the children at once," she ordered, "and then get rid of their mother!"

Heartbroken at her command, the cook brought a large butcher's knife out to the garden where children were playing. They ran toward him, their pretty little faces trusting and happy. One look at them and he knew he could never kill them. Horrified by the queen's cruelty and by what she had asked him to do, he confessed everything to the princess.

The princess did not lose heart. She immediately sent the fastest messenger to warn the prince. As soon as he heard the news, the prince turned his army over to the leadership of a faithful general and he raced home as fast as his horse could carry him. After questioning the cook, the prince knew at once what he had to do.

He immediately banished the cruel queen to a far-off land where she could no longer cause any harm. Everyone else lived happily for the rest of their days.

This is the end of the story.
Now close the book,
turn it upside down,
and you can begin another tale.

Heading in the direction of the noise, they wandered through the woods until they came to a clearing. Then they saw what was making such a racket. Another giant had just

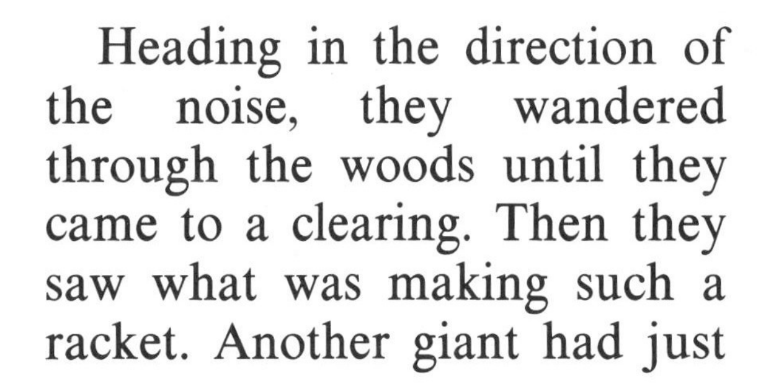

uprooted five or six trees at one time with his bare hands. It was hard work and he was hot and sweaty, but he didn't seem to mind.

"What are you doing?" asked the soldier.

"Oh, just chores, my friend. I'm collecting firewood."

"This strong man could be very handy to have around," the soldier thought, and asked the new giant to join them.

"Sure, why not?" the tree giant said, the trees clutched in his arms. "But wait just a minute." He tossed the trees over his shoulder, with such force that they landed with their roots back in the ground. "Okay. Let's go."

This is the end of the story.
Now close the book,
turn it upside down,
and you can begin another tale.

The king was not pleased. He summoned his best general.

"Follow those thieves and bring back my treasure!" he thundered loudly. The general marched off with a powerful army. The soldier and the six giants were already far into the forest, dividing the fortune. Suddenly, the sharp-eyed giant jumped up.

"There's an army heading this way," he warned. "They might be coming for our treasure."

"Well, they won't succeed! laughed the nasal giant. He removed his hand from his nose and sneezed. Men, horses, and weapons flew through the air like leaves in the wind. They landed right back where they had started, in front of a very disappointed king who wanted an explanation.

The soldier and the six giants divided the treasure equally and then each went his own way, rich and happy.

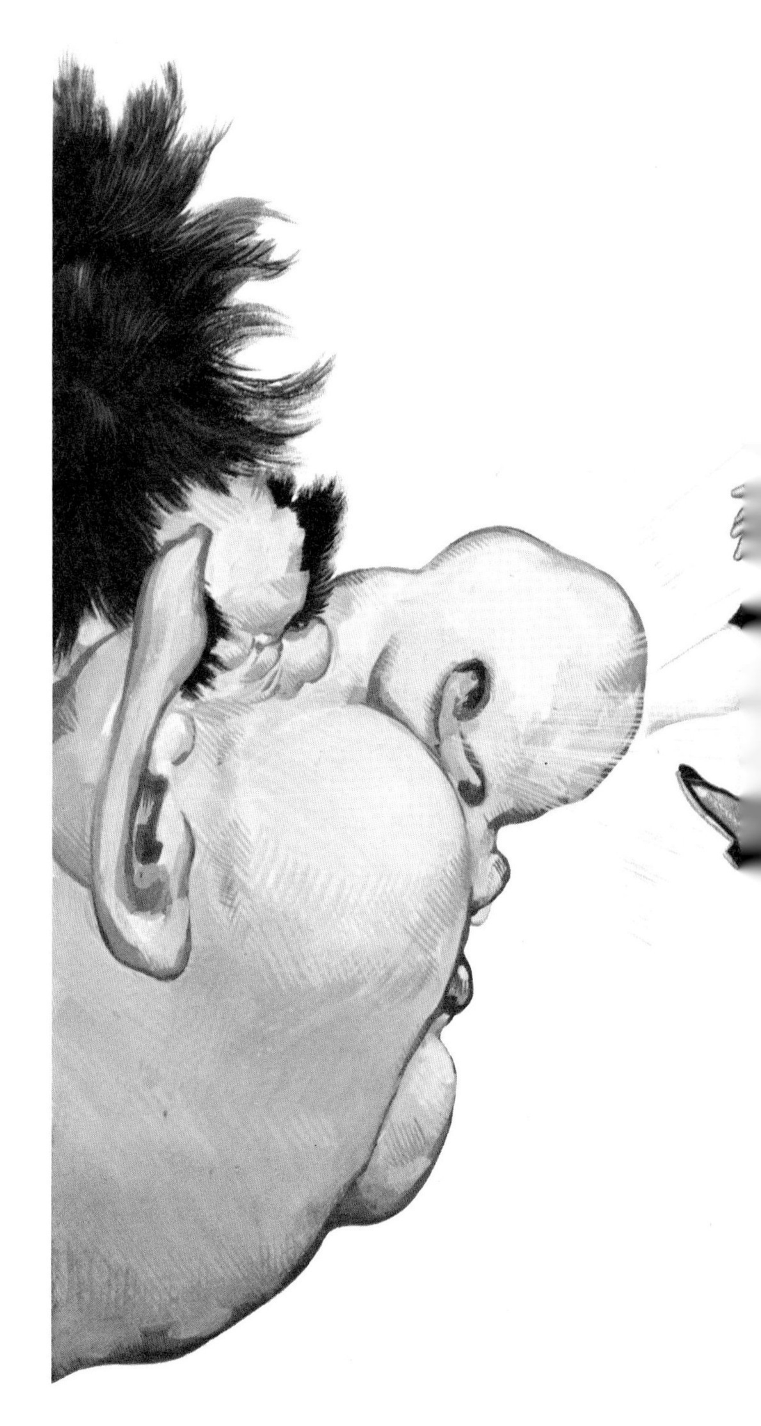

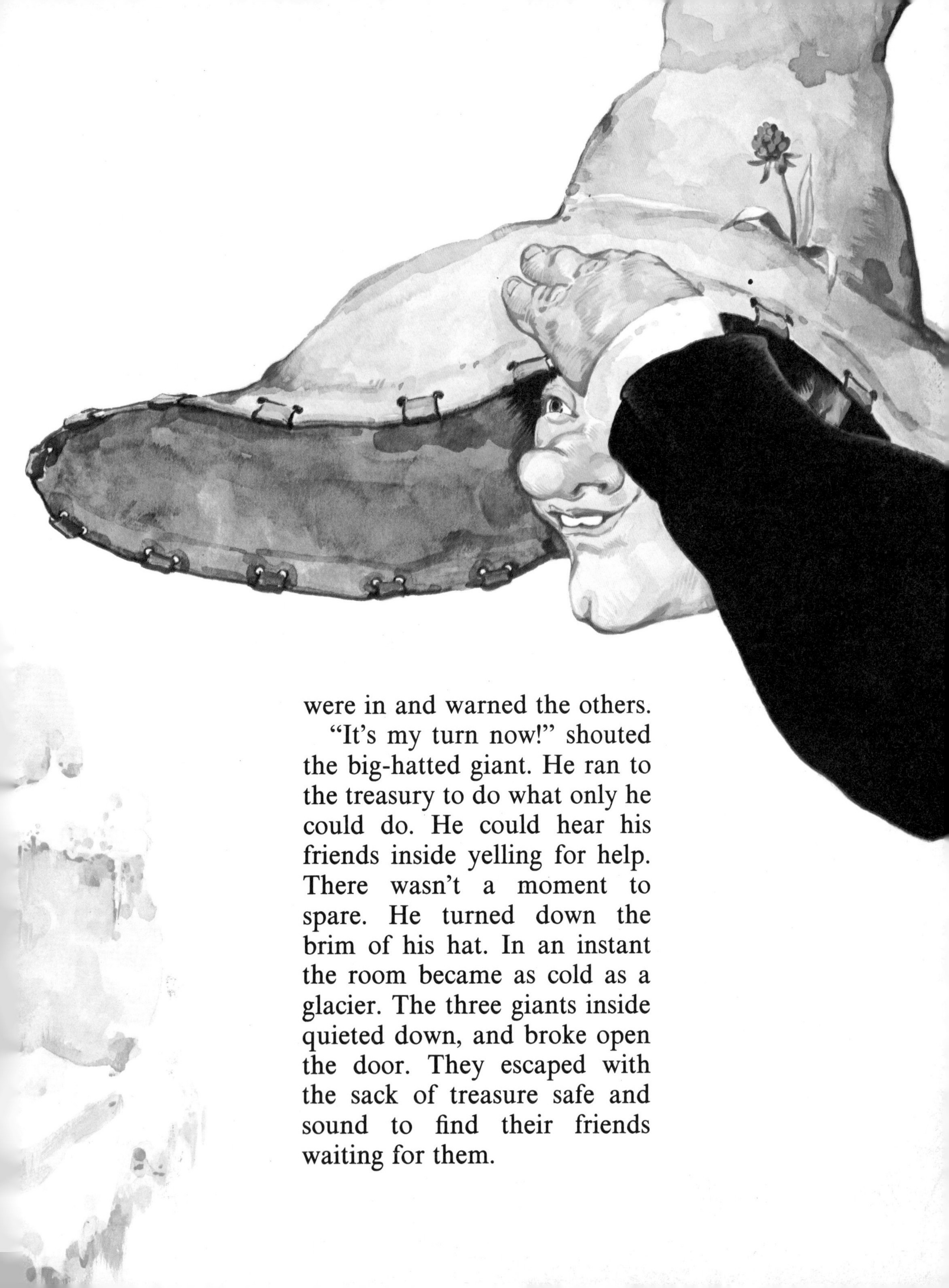

were in and warned the others.

"It's my turn now!" shouted the big-hatted giant. He ran to the treasury to do what only he could do. He could hear his friends inside yelling for help. There wasn't a moment to spare. He turned down the brim of his hat. In an instant the room became as cold as a glacier. The three giants inside quieted down, and broke open the door. They escaped with the sack of treasure safe and sound to find their friends waiting for them.

When the king was told what was happening he lost his temper. True, he had given his word as a king, but there are limits! He ordered a huge fire to be built under the royal treasury floor so that the giants would be roasted alive and the treasure would be safe.

They were about to leave the room, when it became unbearably hot. They tried to escape with the fortune but the smoke was so thick that they couldn't find the door.

Their sharp-eyed companion was again watching over his friends. He saw the danger they

can go to the palace and claim the princess!" he said to the fleet-footed giant.

The giant did as he was told. The king, however, was not too thrilled with the idea of allowing his daughter to get married to a giant.

"If you renounce your right to marry my daughter," the king offered, "I will give you as much treasure as you can carry with you. What do you say?"

The fleet-footed giant was not particularly interested in getting married anyway. "Could I bring two friends to help me?" he asked. The king hesitated a moment, then agreed.

The fleet-footed giant summoned his two strongest friends–the boulder giant and the tree giant. Together they brought a sack large enough to hold a house. The king was nervous, but a king must keep his word. He ordered the guards to take the giants to the royal treasury. As the guards watched in disbelief, the giants filled the sack with gold, precious stones, and jewels until there was nothing left of the treasure the king had taken a lifetime to accumulate.

him, running as fast as a gazelle.

Up he jumped and off he ran. He passed entire fields and villages in a single stride. He caught up with the princess, overtook her, and entered the town square without a drop missing from his bucket. The princess crossed the finish line half an hour later, thoroughly furious.

The soldier was grinning and prancing around. "Now you

“Don’t worry about a thing,” said the eagle-eyed giant, “leave everything to me.” He loaded his rifle, aimed, and fired. His bullet struck the tree just a few inches from the sleeping fleet-footed giant’s head. Flying wood splinters and cracking branches awoke him with a start. He looked around in bewilderment, and saw the princess miles head of

footed giant was every bit as fast as he had claimed. He reached the fountain in no time, filled his bucket, and started back. But he was not used to waking up at dawn. He was so sure that he would win the race that he stopped to take a brief nap under a tree. He slept so soundly that he did not notice the princess passing by, once with her bucket empty and again with her bucket full.

His friends were not asleep, though. They were on the alert. The sharp-eyed giant was, of course, the lookout, and immediately realized what was happening.

"Our friend is sound asleep and the princess is winning!" he informed the others.

"We've got to wake him up!" they shouted.

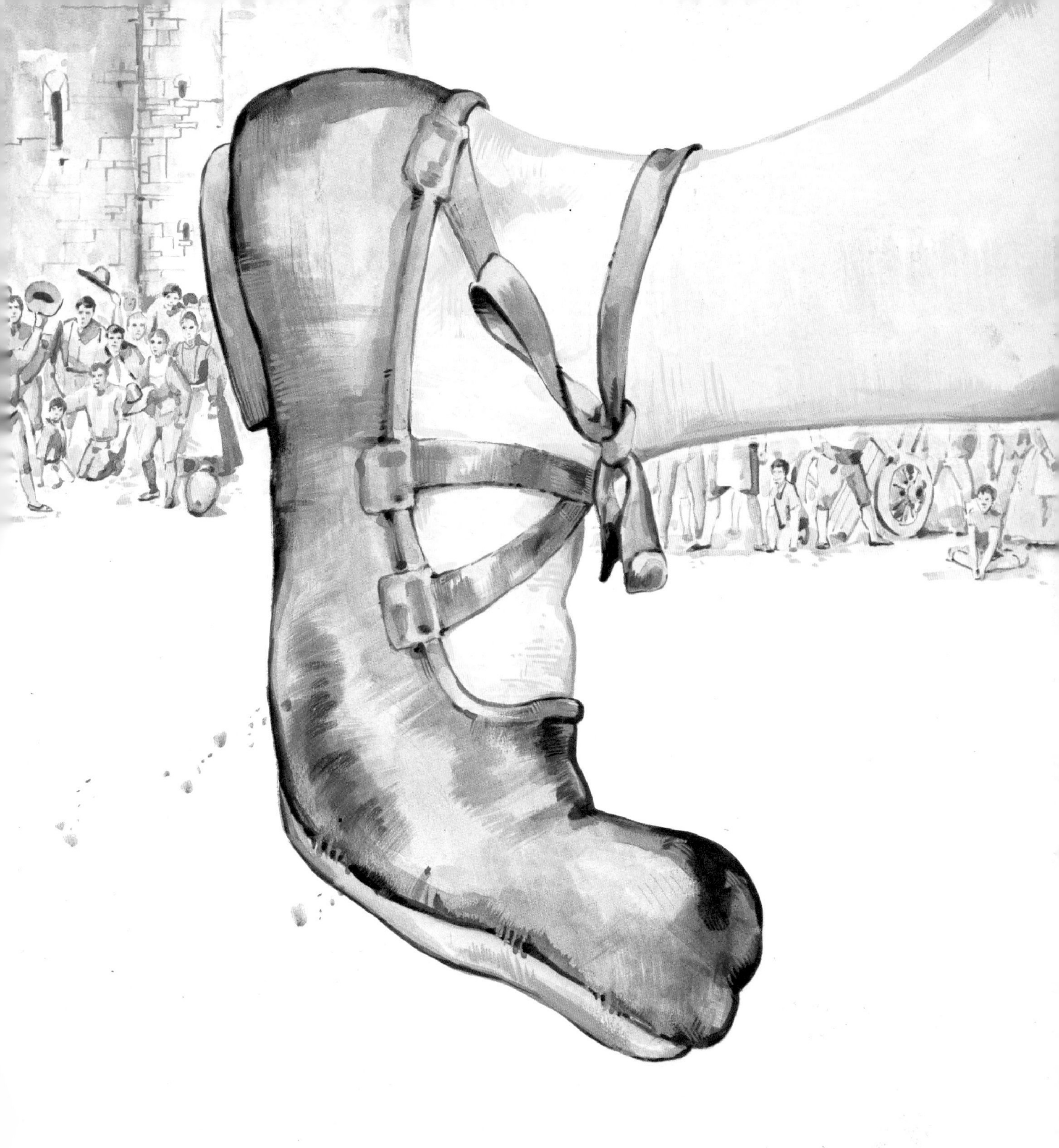

tentions at the royal palace. The king decreed that the race would be held the very next day.

The beautiful princess and the giant, who had untied his ankles, set off at dawn with empty buckets. The fleet-

They came to a town where the streets were filled with people making a great commotion. It didn't take long to find out why. The king's daughter had announced that she would marry any man who could beat her in a footrace. The contest was not as easy as it seemed. The princess ran as swiftly as a hare. The contestants had to run carrying a bucket of water back from a fountain in a distant village without spilling a drop. Everyone was sure the princess would win, if someone were daring enough to try.

The soldier and his six giant friends talked about the race. The fleet-footed giant declared that he would be happy to take part in it. He announced his in-

each other, but it was too difficult to hold a conversation this way and they soon tired of it. So, when they saw a small field they stopped to chat, have a drink, and rest for a while so they would have energy for adventures to come.

While they were relaxing another giant came by, a young one with a strange hopping walk. He was smiling as he hopped nearer. When he got close they saw that his ankles were tied together with a rope. He looked like an overgrown child playing hopscotch.

The soldier walked right up to him and asked, "Why are you walking like that? Doesn't it make you tired?"

The young giant shrugged his shoulders. "It's the only thing I can do. If I untied my ankles I would find myself at the end of the world in a flash."

"That's fast!" the soldier exclaimed with admiration. "Hey, you're as unusual as the rest of us. Why not join us and seek your fortune in the big world?"

"I think I'd like that," the fleet-footed giant answered, and off they all went.

"A catastrophe?!" the others all wondered aloud.

"Yes. A catastrophe. The shadow from the brim of my hat makes the land freeze solid. Wherever I have gone with my hat brim turned down has become like the North Pole."

"I see," the soldier said, very impressed. "Listen, we're traveling the world to find luck and adventure. You're welcome to join us if you'd like. Someone like you doesn't come along every day."

"That would be great!" said the big-hatted giant. "I've been rather bored just standing here."

"Now we are six, the soldier chuckled. "My friends, let us each put our best foot forward. The world is ours!" They ran to the road but it was narrow at that point and they had to walk single file. They tried talking to

"You should come with us," the soldier suggested, and the nasal giant gladly accepted. The five of them marched down the road in high spirits.

The sun was beginning to set when they approached another giant. His clothes were rather plain, but he wore a fine hat with a wide brim which was turned back. He stood near a bridge, scuffing his shoes in the dirt.

"Why are you wearing your hat like that?" the soldier shouted as they came nearer. "I know the sun is setting, but it's still pretty strong." The soldier thought he would never understand why giants behaved so strangely.

The big-hatted giant gave a great sigh. "I have no choice. If I lowered the brim I'd cause a catastrophe."

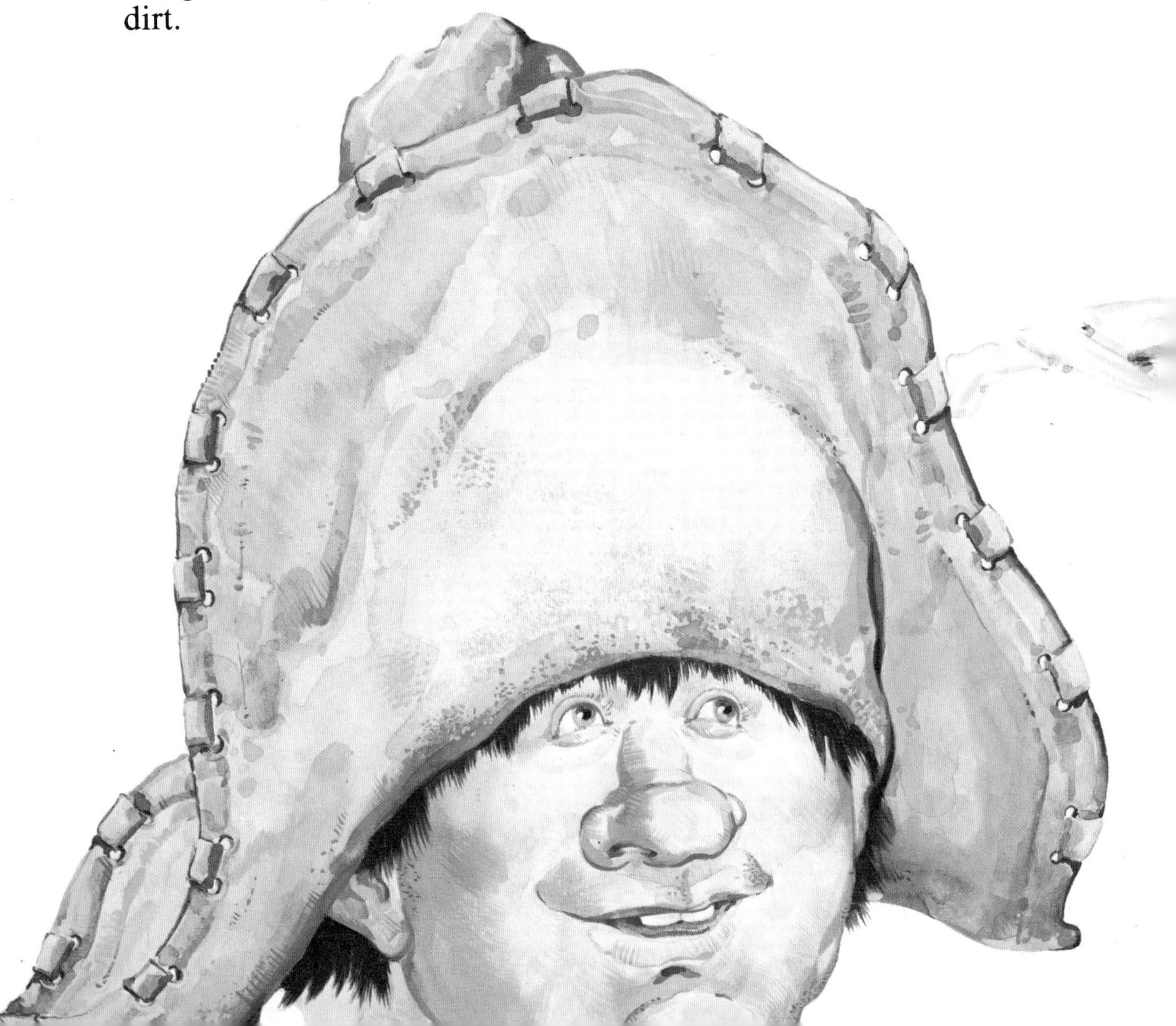

They had hardly begun walking when this sharp-eyed giant saw something in the distance. They continued in that direction until the rest of them could see what he saw—a huge man, sitting on a fallen tree, tightly pinching his nose.

"Why are you doing that?" the soldier wanted to know.

"I have to!" he said in a voice that sounded funny because he was holding his nose. "If I sneezed I would blow away everything for miles around—people, animals, trees, houses, everything!"

eye!" the soldier said. Just then the giant fired, and a few seconds later they heard a horse whinnying contentedly from afar. "You should come with us to search for fun, fame, and fortune in the big world."

"Sounds like a good opportunity," the eagle-eyed giant said. "What are we waiting for?"

As soon as they stepped out of the forest they nearly tripped over another giant, aiming his gun. They couldn't understand what he was trying to hit because there were no targets or small animals around.

"What are you aiming at?" the soldier asked him.

"That horse over there, in the field," the giant pointed out the animal standing far off on the horizon. "Well, not the horse, actually, but that fly on his tail that's been bothering him all day."

"Wow! What an amazing

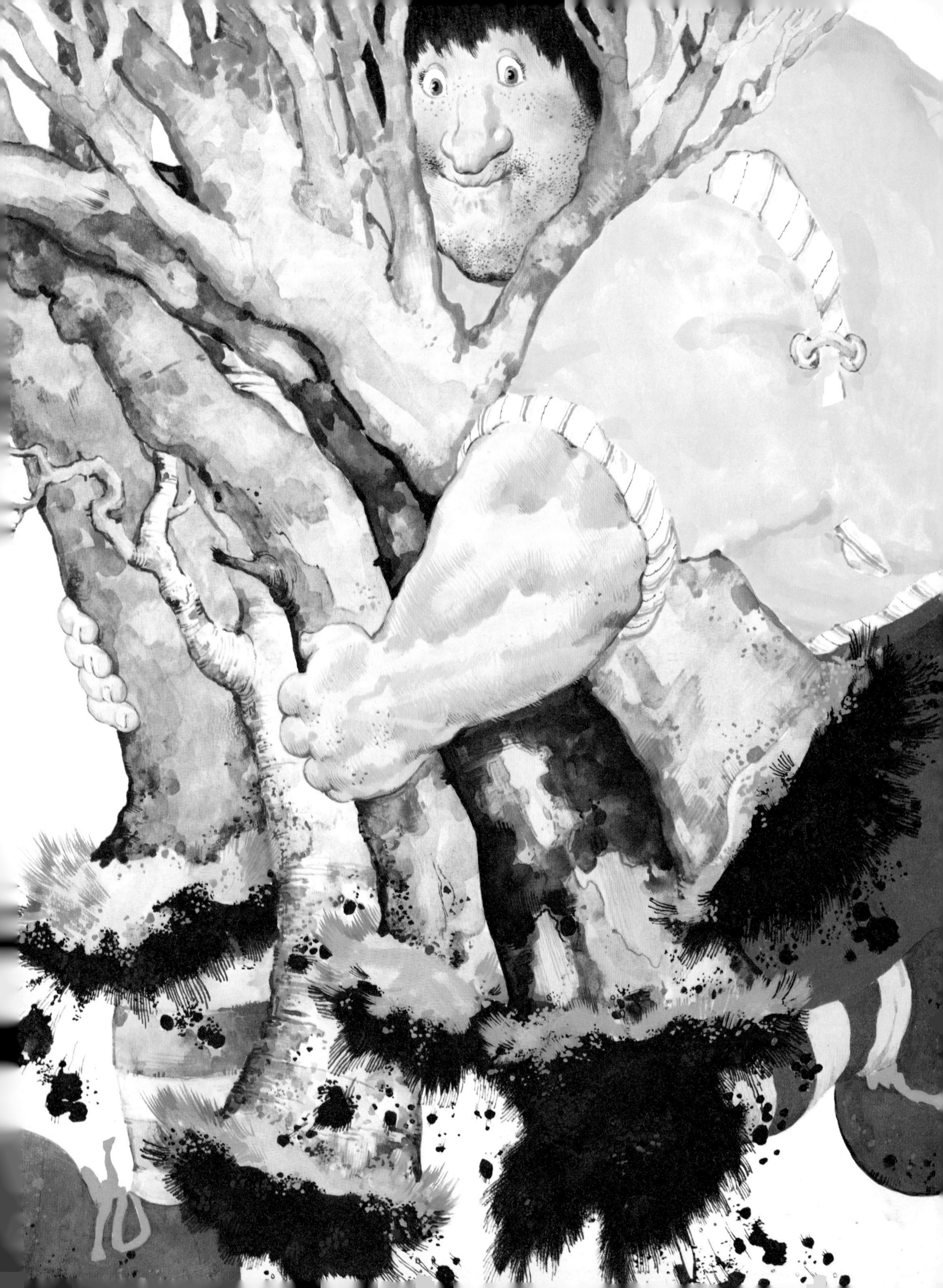

ing a secret. "If I let go, it would thunder down the mountainside and crush that village to smithereens."

"You must be mighty strong," the soldier said, looking from the boulder to the village far below, and back to the giant. "Do you want to come with me? I'm going out into the world to seek my fortune. I bet that we would make a great team."

The giant thought about how dull it was to stand in one place and brace a rock with his arms. "I think you're right," he said. He let the boulder go. It rolled and bounced so hard that it changed the shape of the mountain in several places. What a waste of time it had been for the giant to hold back the boulder! It bounced right over the village without breaking so much as a fencepost.

And so they set off on their travels, the soldier appearing to be a midget next to the giant. During the trip, they argued constantly about which road to take, but the soldier always won because the whole thing had been his idea in the first place.

They were walking along the edge of a forest and telling jokes to each other when they heard a strange, loud noise from somewhere deep among the trees.

"What's that?" the soldier asked, tilting his head to one side so that he could hear better.

"I don't know," said the adventurous giant, "but we could find out."

THE SOLDIER AND THE SIX GIANTS

Once upon a time there was a soldier who had no work because everyone had been at peace for some time. He thought and thought about what he should do. Finally, he decided to explore the world and see what else it had to offer. He began to walk.

He had just settled into a comfortable pace, fast enough to get somewhere but slow enough to see where he was, when he came upon a curious sight. A giant stood at the very edge of a steep, high cliff, holding up a huge boulder with both hands.

"What are you doing?" the soldier asked quietly, afraid he might disturb the giant.

"I'm holding up this rock," the giant replied. He leaned forward as though he were tell-